THESE ROCKS COUNT!

Alison Formento   Illustrated by Sarah Snow

Albert Whitman & Company
Chicago, Illinois

To Alex and Natalie, who make everything in my life count—A.F.

To my mom and dad—S.S.

Library of Congress Cataloging-in-Publication Data is on file with the publisher.

Text copyright © 2014 by Alison Formento.
Illustrations copyright © 2014 by Sarah Snow.
Published in 2014 by Albert Whitman & Company.
ISBN 978-0-8075-7870-4
Printed in China.
10 9 8 7 6 5 4 3 2 1 BP 18 17 16 15 14 13

The design is by Nick Tiemersma.

For more information about Albert Whitman & Company,
visit our web site at www.albertwhitman.com.

Also by Alison Formento
and Sarah Snow

Mr. Tate's class loves taking field trips.
Today they went for a hike.

Everyone stared up at a giant boulder. It was tall—almost as tall as Mr. Tate.

A woman joined them on the path. "Hi, I'm Ranger Pedra. Are you ready to hike and find rocks?"

Shin tightened her shoelaces. "Hiking is fun."

Eli said, "I've got my walking stick."

Jake tried to climb the boulder. "This one is too big for our rock garden."

Natalie stretched on her tiptoes. "Is this the biggest rock in the world?"

Ranger Pedra smiled. "Some rocks are even bigger. They're mountains, like this one."

Mr. Tate held a pebble in the palm of his hand. "They can be tiny too."

Amy kicked a stone into the trees. "Rocks are boring."

"I thought that once too," said Ranger Pedra. She pulled a heavy lump from her backpack.

"It sparkles!" said Natalie.

"This is a geode," said Ranger Pedra. "Rocks don't all shine like this one, but they all have a story inside."

"Rocks don't talk," said Amy.

"They do talk," said Ranger Pedra.

"We have to listen with our eyes and our hands."

She touched the boulder.

Mr. Tate and the children did too.

"What do you feel or see?" asked Mr. Tate.

"I see colors," said Eli.

"It's dirty," said Shin.

"And bumpy," said Natalie.

Ranger Pedra moved her fingers across the boulder. "Every speck is part of this giant rock's journey. It moves and changes just like you."

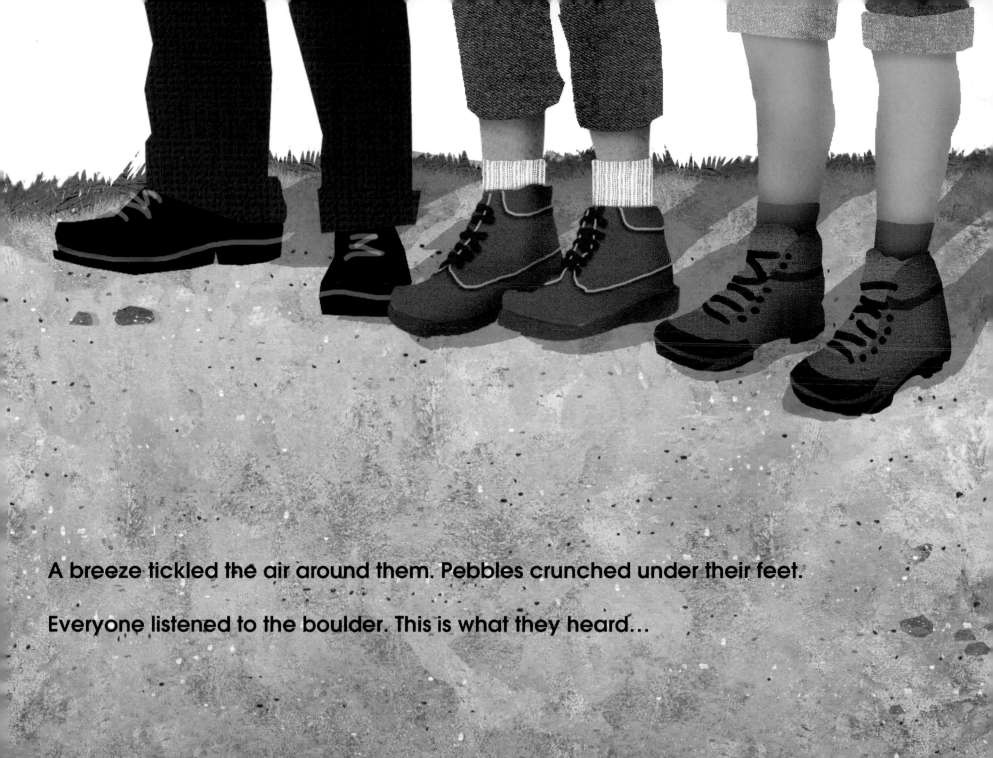

A breeze tickled the air around them. Pebbles crunched under their feet.

Everyone listened to the boulder. This is what they heard…

One sculptor chips and molds, making art from hard stone.

TWO trucks churn cement,
poured for a new building site.

Three busy beetles
chew on moss-covered stones.

Four seaside mounds dry into table salt.

Five hatchlings from a sandy nest,
make tiny turtle trails to the sea.

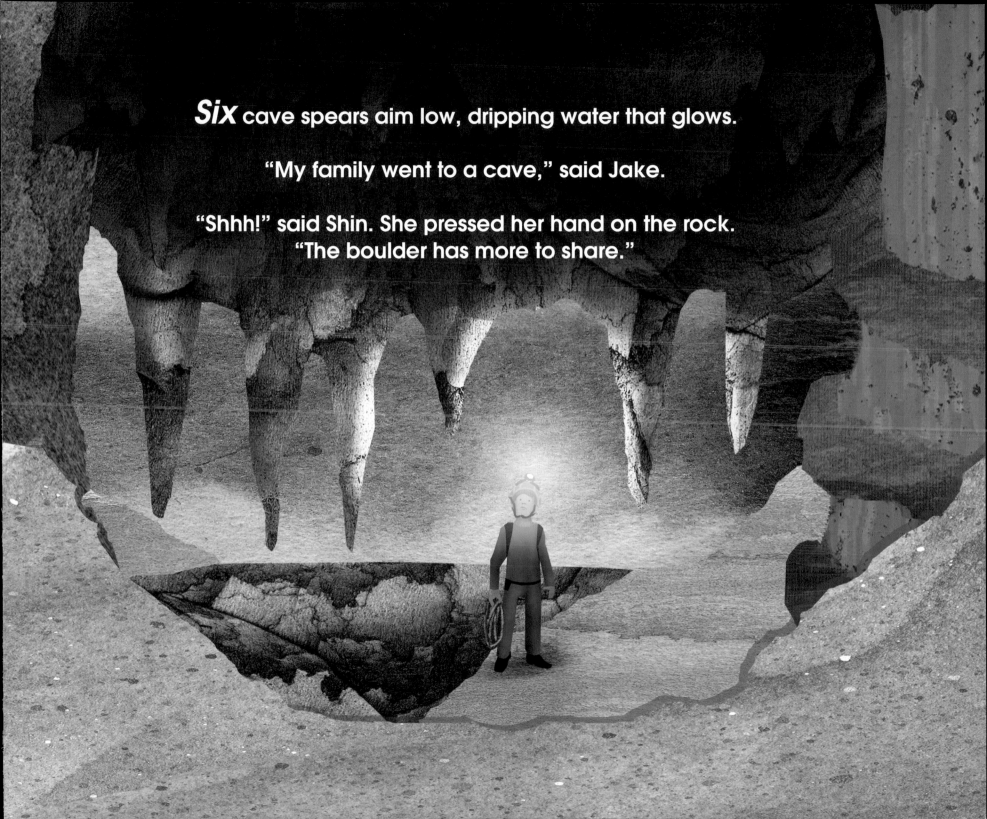

Six cave spears aim low, dripping water that glows.

"My family went to a cave," said Jake.

"Shhh!" said Shin. She pressed her hand on the rock.
"The boulder has more to share."

Seven rough gems, polished bright as stars.

Eight pieces of slate make a nice sidewalk.

Nine
heavy
bricks
stacked
just
right.

Ten panes of glass shine in a new home.

Gems or glass, stone or sand, small or grand,
in water, on land—rocks are nature's building blocks.

"What did you hear?" asked Mr. Tate.

"Rocks count!" said Amy.

"What else is special about rocks?" asked Ranger Pedra.

"Some are shiny," said Natalie.

"Yes, gems for jewelry come from rocks. Rocks can also help tell us about the age of the world."

"How?" asked Shin.

"By looking at rocks in places like the Grand Canyon," said Ranger Pedra.
"Layers of rocks show how much time has passed, just like the rings inside a tree."

"Do you remember when we talked about the rock cycle at school?" asked Mr. Tate.

Shin picked up a handful of pebbles. "That's when rocks change."

"We made up a poem about it." Eli clapped his hands and chanted.

"Hot or cold, wind, snow, and rain—rocks get old, cycle of change."

"Rocks are always changing," said Ranger Pedra. "Just like you." She pointed at the rocks Shin held. "It can take millions of years to form rocks like these."

Mr. Tate sat on a big rock. "Granite is used for building. Can you name some other ways we use rocks?"

For roads," said Natalie.

Jake said, "My mom cooks with rock salt."

"They're building a new statue at the library," said Amy.

"Rocks and minerals are used inside phones and computers too." said Mr. Tate.

"What about cars and airplanes?" asked Eli. "Or trains?"

Ranger Pedra nodded. "Rocks and minerals are even used to make toothpaste."

"Wow!" said Amy. "There's more to rocks than I thought."

Ranger Pedra smiled. "Now you're ready to identify rocks."

Mr. Tate showed them a rock guide. "We'll take pictures of what we find."

The class hiked up Rocky Ridge Mountain. They searched, found, and photographed...

One, two, three,
four, five, six,
seven, eight, nine,
ten different kinds of rocks.

On the hike down the mountain, they stopped at the big boulder.

Jake patted the huge rock. "Thanks for sharing your story."

"And for the great things you give us," said Shin.

"Like shiny gems," said Natalie.

Amy gently touched the boulder. "Rocks aren't boring at all. I'm sorry I said that."

Ranger Pedra smiled.

A breeze blew and a few stones skittered down the mountain path.

Eli climbed onto the boulder. "Rocks rock!"

Why rocks rock...

Rocks are everywhere! They are under our homes, our schools, and beneath the soil under our feet when we walk outside. Rocks are what Earth's crust is made of and they change in an ongoing cycle just like water. During this cycle, rocks are heated and melted. Then they cool and harden, compress and compact, weather and erode. Three types of rocks are formed during the rock cycle:

- Igneous means made from heat. Magma, or melted rock under Earth's crust, comes to the surface as lava and cools. *Examples: granite, quartz, basalt*
- Sedimentary rocks, like those found in the Grand Canyon, form from sediments through erosion. *Examples: sandstone, limestone, clay*
- Metamorphic means change. These rocks change inside Earth's crust through heat, pressure, and chemical activity. *Examples: marble, slate, and gneiss*

Scientists called geologists study Earth's rocks, big and small, to better understand how our planet changes every day. Much of what we know about Earth's past comes from how rocks have been used throughout time. Primitive tools such as grindstones, knives, and spears used by early man were made of rocks. Ancient temples, pyramids, statues, and the first roads discovered in Rome were also built from rocks.

Today we still travel on roads, walk on sidewalks, live, learn, and work in buildings made from rocks. Beautiful statues and monuments such as the Martin Luther King Jr. Memorial are carved from stone. Computers, telephones, televisions, and machinery including airplanes, trains, ships, and cars are all manufactured with materials created from rocks and minerals. Salt, toothpaste, and even the lead in your pencil are all made from rocks and minerals. Rocks star in our lives!

Some rocks are so big that people from all over the world go to visit them. A few of the biggest are the Rock of Gibraltar, Ayers Rock, and the Blarney Stone. Famous rock formations include the sandstone wonders of Arches National Park in Utah, the basalt blocks of the Giant's Causeway off the coast of Ireland, and stunning Shilin Stone Forest in China.

While giant rocks attract sightseers, geologists are most interested in studying how these rocks were first formed. That means looking beneath Earth's crust. Whenever a volcano erupts or the earth shakes, the world's rocky crust shifts and changes. Billions of years of earthquakes and volcanic activity helped form our world's continents, mountain ranges, and canyons. Scientists who study earthquakes are called seismologists and those who study volcanoes are volcanists.

Volcanoes are vents in Earth's crust where lava, steam, and ash are expelled. Some volcanoes, like Eyjafjallajökull, which powerfully erupted in Iceland in 2010, spew enough ash to disrupt air travel. Other volcanoes continually erupt, like those in Hawaii, where visitors can view molten rock up close and scientists track and measure slow-flowing lava. Over time, this lava will harden and cool, adding new usable land for animals and people.

Humans need rocks for building, and in nature, rocks also help shelter wildlife. Boulders and rocky caves provide protection and homes for creatures, whether they live deep in the ocean like an octopus or in the highest cliffs like mountain goats. Insects, birds, and reptiles nest under and around rocks and many plants and trees thrive in a rocky habitat.

Pick up a pebble in your yard and think about how it was first melted rock under the ground. If you're hiking, imagine the "rock-ibilities"—tools, electronics, buildings, and more—that could be created from the boulders under your feet. After you brush your teeth with toothpaste, smile wide because you know how much these rocks count!